Indigo League

Poems Inspired by Pokemon Trainers

Written by RJ Walker

Table of Contents

My Mother Explains My Depression to Me
(After Sabrina Benaim)

There was a great storm at sea
The disciples were afraid the ship would get swallowed up
now read
read
read what Jesus said
read it
he said
"Why are ye fearful, O ye of little faith?"
Then he arose, and rebuked the winds and the sea;
and there was a great calm.

See
she says
See
Don't you feel better?

and she does not know
that I tried to drown myself
accidentally on purpose
for the 2nd time today.
but that is too much to say
so instead I say
No
I am not Jesus
and I have depression, not a storm

She says
We all know doctors just make that up in order to sell pills
We all know you just made this whole thing up
to get out of going on your mission
You don't have depression
you just don't have enough faith
Jesus said so

but it's ok
look, keep reading,
about the two men, possessed with devils
They say
"If thou cast us out, suffer us to go away into the herd of swine."

And Jesus says "GO" and sends them into the swine
and they drowned
they drowned
that's why It's ok.
        She holds my head underwater and says
Because it wasn't you
you got a devil in you
so we get it out
and you can stop with that limping
and storming yourself to death
and go back on your mission
teach those folks in Texas
about the Jesus who saved you
from the devil you got in you.
We'll baptize it out of you
yeah, yeah
I know it. I know it to be true. I Prayed about it
it's the truth
the truth

The truth is a drowned pig
a ship at sea.

You are His tool, RJ
Jesus doesn't let his tools rust
not like your father
because we all know I didn't give this to you
this sad boy disease you made up
the devil you got in you
with his cigarettes
and corona
So I'm gonna divorce this devil out of you
yup yup it works
worked for me

        I say
I don't want to be Jesus' drowned pig
        I say
I want to die
        But I fail to want myself to death

        but she comes close when She says

you WILL fulfill your purpose
Kill the parts of yourself that are yourself

        I say
        I'm trying
        she says

You,
You are the anti-christ
Jesus said so
Keep reading look
look, look what jesus said
he says
"Your son is a broken ship at sea
and he keeps trying to splinter himself
because he hates Me
he hates God
He hates You."

How could you do this to me?
After everything I've done
taught you how to be a blade
so stop goshdang cutting yourself

How dare you hurt me with your hurt
How dare you Kill Jesus with your killing.
He died your death to death and now you can't die
so you can't get away

        I say, in the voice of all my suicide attempts
        each one a pig,
        a shipwreck
        Drowned at sea
What have we to do with thee, oh son of god
art thou come hither to torment us before the time?

She hands me the whole violent ocean and says
Go then,
You vile thing,
I will not have you in this home that is your home
I will not have you die in this coffin that is your room
because it was never your room
all this

all this was mine,

it was mine and I gave it to you

wretched beast
I cannot bear the sight of you
my son who has eaten my son
and wears his bones
I take back my motherhood
and give you stones,
no go forth into the swines
and drown.
"GO"

She waits for me to respond.
But I have too much to say.
Yet I manage to say it all.
in a single word.

Goodbye.

Youngster

In those days,
I was not a boy.
I was a match.

I was a little red cherry
with a whole bonfire inside of me
waiting to burn the world down.

But I didn't.
I'll never forgive myself
for that.

Bug Catcher

How terrifying it must be
to be a bug.
To be you.
To be prey for everything that isn't you.
So small you can't even fight back
before becoming a snack
or a stain.

I will save all of you.
Don't worry.
Don't be scared.
You'll find it's much safer for you here
in my jaws.

Lass

I got you this

    A rock?

It's not a rock, it's a door

    If it's a door, where does it lead?

To me.

Emmigration Canyon

It's not the fall

that kills you.

It's the view.

from the top of the cliff.

It teaches you
to romanticize dying
the way teenagers do
when they tell half truths
about sleepovers
and drive up the canyon
to kiss each other to death.

But tonight
you've long shed your teenage bones
And you're driving up the same canyon
alone and
you stand
on the
edge.

And you see the view.
You forget the word "alone" exists
because, out there
is the whole world.

So close
        you could
                kiss it

So you do,
like a teenager.

And all the hate you have for yourself
explodes like a firecracker

into the great black sea below.

The ripples
lapping at the feet of the world, and everyone in it.
They all sing

    "How dare you
    How dare you romanticize death
    instead of us."

They are just
jealous
of the view.

Brock

I'm a rock salesman.
Actually,
that's not entirely true.

People don't buy the rocks
they buy the secrets inside of the rocks.
Indeed
I sell the finest rocks
with the finest secrets
in Pewter City.

But it's not just
the shiniest rock
that has the best secret.
No, no.
It's how the rock learned the secret
that makes the stone precious.

Take a look
at this brown chunk of granite.
It learned how to end a fight
when she pushed it
through the back
of her husband's skull.

And this smooth stone
learned the 5 words
that will make anybody
fall in love with you for a day
by catching an engagement ring
that was tossed into the river.

This rock, though,
this rock is not for sale.
This rock learned
Where my father went
on the day
my mother dove headfirst
onto it like a feather pillow
And never woke up.

Blackbelt

I can break bricks
with my forehead.

I broke myself
enough times,
I learned how to
break anything.

I can't punch
my way out
this time.
You know I tried.

I'm sorry.
I love you.
But don't forgive me.

Beauty

You think of love
as a battle
silly boy.

That would imply
there is a loser.
If so-
then that loser
would be you.

Hiker

The higher
you climb up a mountain,
the harder it is to breathe.

The further you fall in love,
the harder it is to exist.

This why I hike mountains
instead of hearts.

Castles Made of Sand

I found him locked in his friend's car
after the concert
on his back.
In medicine, we call this position "supine."
A fallen tree
carried downstream
by the rapids.

I had to break the window to get to him.
When I did
the whole Snake River
poured out
of the car
from his lungs
hissing and rattling and venomous.
White water and all.
Headed toward the ocean.

Our drunk goldfish floats
belly up.
Staring into a quickly approaching sky,
perhaps thinking of you, Jimi.

When you kissed the sky,
Was it like you had always described?
Or was it a numbness that would make the Sandman jealous.
Did you feel like a sandcastle
Dissolving into the ocean?
Slowly slipping away.

It is a terrifying helplessness
To drown without limbs.
Just like that boy,
Your stomach and lungs switched jobs.

But I guess there are those who prefer their rock stars dead.
If you survived past the age of 27,
You must not have been rocking hard enough.

At what point did "Jimi's only fun when he's on something,"
Become "Jimi's only Jimi when he's on something."
Maybe sober Jimi didn't know how to play guitar,
But I bet sober Jimi knew how to breathe.

You were not the first artist to drown on dry land:
F. Scott Fitzgerald, Billie Holiday, Jack Kerouac, Brian Jones.

And you weren't the last:
Bon Scott, John Bonham, Whitney Houston, Amy Winehouse
And 80,000 Americans per year
4,700 of which are children
Like the boy I found in the parking lot of that show.
Locked in the car.
Drowned.

And I bet that they were all buried supine.
belly up and carried to the ocean.
To be drowned by gravity forever.

And so castles made of sand
Slips into the sea
Eventually.
Some sooner than others.

Misty

I've never been afraid
of drowning.
I've never been afraid
of anything, really.
But especially not drowning.

I've never been afraid
of heights either.
And so,
having no fear
of heights or drowning
I have decided to become a diver.

Brock told me about his mother,
the diver.
How beautiful she looked
falling like a stone feather.
Plunging toward the great black sea.

I think that's what made me
fall in love with the water
and the cold air above it.
I think that's why I've built this diving board
out of all the things I'm not afraid of.
This trembling plank of ice
which I have built my body on.

At midnight
I stand on the edge
and ask myself
If I'm ready to be a diver.
"Not yet"
says Brock's Mom
from the great black sea below
and I am afraid.

Sailor

So tonight,
I will give you a ship.
I will not buy you one,
I will not build you one,
I will become one.
I will swim the sea gone.
I will be yours.

So, Hero,
smile me a house fire.
Smile me a lighthouse.
Smile me back to shore
with that candle of yours.

Swimmer

In the morning,
I stood on the beach
waiting
for Leander.
His shipwrecked body
washed up on shore.
Limbs splintered into pieces
mast, broken in two places,
he was waterlogged
and scuttled.
If only I had kept my candle lit.
The cargo in his chest,
was still intact.
I took it into my arms.
It was a heavy
and precious
anchor.
I tied it to my chest
and threw myself into the sea.

For what is love,
but another form of drowning.

Fisherman

Oh!
A Bite!
Feels like a big one
like the whole sea
has my hook in it's teeth.

But I am an expert fisherman
I know how to tire a thing out.

Get the net!
Drag it onto shore!
What manner of sea monster
did my line snag this time?

Oh,
It's another broken heart.
This is the last time
I use my feelings as bait.

The City of Sunsets

The sun never sets here
but it is always setting.
So the city lives forever.
You wonder why
everyone doesn't just move here
and become immortal.

      "That's not how it works"
Says the woman with the oxygen tank,
aged but ageless.

"The people are always setting here
but they never set.
always dying
but never dead.
Same as anywhere.

      Stand on the pier where the dusk is brightest
      you will see what I mean.
You'll experience the sunset of your lifetime."

And so you stand on the pier
and become swallowed by the orange light,
just like she said to do.

You should be feeling
your own sunset reaching for you.
Old age creeping.
Aching bones. Memory loss.

But you don't feel anything.
You just stand there and bleed.
It terrifies you.

Lt. Surge

The thing they don't tell you
when they send you to war
is the Enemy's favorite color.

They don't mention
their favorite flavor
of ice cream, either.

Come to think of it
they didn't once tell me
the enemy's favorite song.
Or at least their favorite band.

I think that's a shame, really.
How am I supposed to fly a mission
without the proper intel?

You know,
I think a war would be much easier to wage
If everyone knew
everybody else's favorite song.
I think it would give a tactical advantage
to everybody, all around.

But what do I know
I'm just a soldier
with a pair of headphones
that tried to hang himself
with them.
Ain't got nothin' to do
with how I pulled them off his corpse.
Ain't got nothing to do with how I killed him.
Ain't got nothing to do
with how much I love
the music he was listening to.

I think, if they'd have given me that intel,
this war
and that war
and that war
would have been won
by The Beatles
a long time ago.

Rocker

To be a musician
is to be a god
that nobody gives a shit about.

To be a roadie
is to be an angel
to a god
with at least a cult following.

To be a record label
is to be an entire religion
that makes up its own gods
whenever tithing needs to be paid.

Scientist

I could not have you
so I built you.

A shiny,
exact
holographic replica
of you.

I finally turned you on
and you immediately
rejected me.

And I knew
my exact replica
was a success.

Engineer

It's unplugged.
It's been unplugged this whole time.
I can't believe this
I spent hours trying to work out
exactly what was wrong,
following the troubleshooting instructions
to the letter,
and it was just unplugged.

You're right.
You're right.
I should have listened to you
from the beginning.

There
fixed it.
We should be able
to get pregnant now.

Lavender Town

A Seance for the Boy I Let Die

If there are any spirits present
they may make themselves known.

I know you're there
dead boy.
I know you're there
because I carry you everywhere
Even this place
so full of life and stories.

I took philosophy in high school.
        My teacher taught us the Trolley problem.
There is a runaway train barreling down the tracks. Ahead, there are five people tied up and
unable to move. You are standing some distant train yard, next to a lever that switches the
train to a different track. But there is a single person on the other track.
Never has a lever felt more like a trigger
Never has a wristband felt more like a noose

To be a medic
is to be a campfire
a thing that holds ghost stories.
And I cannot speak yours
without smoke in my throat.

I'm sorry, dead boy
You were just on the other set of tracks
It is so much easier to think of you as a philosophical debate
hipsters have over coffee
A meme you scroll past on the internet
and not a body
that I must carry.

To work triage
is to decide the priority
of who gets treated.
It is to volunteer to pull the lever
knowing that your body
is also on both sets of tracks.

I wear a black wristband
every day
since I put one on you.
You must know by now
that in triage
a black wristband
is a deathmark.
It means that this person

is triaged as a corpse
or not worth saving.
I wear it on my right wrist
It hides the cuts
without hiding my desire for death.

We only had the one defibrillator
And a room full of broken heartbeats
inside kids
who took the wrong medicine
at the wrong show.

I knew I'd be throwing another log
on this ghost story heart,
and that log was you
and it's been burning me awake ever since.

I bring you here now,
to ask
one dead boy
to another
not for forgiveness
but OF forgiveness.

Is it even a word
in the language of the dead?
Can it even fit in my mouth yet,
does it sound like the girl
who lived instead of you
is it her name?
or her patched up heartbeat?

Or is it the shriek of your mother
the quiet rage of your father?
Does it sound like this black bracelet
or my pulse beneath it?

Do you hear him?
He says
        A train is coming.

The Atomic Arcade Kid

You see a run down arcade at the center of the city
which is also at the center of the world.
You've got twenty bucks in quarters.
Quarters are the prayer of coins, you know.
The pocket change people hang onto
just in case.

You bring these prayers into the shitty arcade
that has no right to exist
in the world of triple A MMORPG and FPS titles.
You go here because you also
feel as though you have no right to exist.

The screen on Defender shows the face of a missing child
and you know that you are the missing child.
A child missing from it's body
who wandered out of the tall grass
and into this purgatory of fuzzy screens.

Missing:
8 Years Old
Last Seen
February 1999.
Brown Hair
Brown Eyes
Keen Eye for the wondrous.
Holds the high score.
Has the power
to be greater than you.
Which is possibly the reason
why they are missing.
Bring them back.
Safely, and better than you found them.
There is a reward.
It is a type of fire.

you see this ad
and immediately
combust.

Erika

You know,
we're the real flowers here.
The plants are the ones
that arrange us
and place us
so neatly on the dinner table.

Notice the tree in the park
and its arrangement of lovers?
Or the corn in the field
and its arrangement of laborers.

I'd like to think of myself
as a potted plant
that sits near the window
which they water
and feed
and is too pretty to cut.

But I see them
harvesting humans
like it's a full moon
in autumn.
Planting them in the dirt
and feasting on their rotting bones.
And I wonder
when I whither into a corpse
and the bugs come for my leaves
will they consume me, like the rest?

I bring these concerns up
with the oak tree in my yard.
He doesn't say anything.
But the wind blows
and I know
he is hungry.

Super Nerd

I've been roleplaying
my way through life
since elementary school.

One time
I role played myself
through college
and got an degree.

One time
I role played myself
through a job interview
and got hired.

One time
I role-played myself
as yours
and I bled to death.

Jr. Trainer

In boy scouts
they taught us
all kinds of knots.

So, when you said
you wanted to tie the knot with me,
I was expecting a square knot
or a clove hitch
or at least something
other than
a noose.

But my answer is yes.

Tamer

Doesn't the whip
feel so good?
I think so.

I can see you judging me,
your silent disgust, as you watch.

But come here, feel it for yourself.
Press the whip into your palm.
hear the screams of the beasts
as they obey your thunder.
I promise
you will never want to let go.

Albatross

OK, so
Albatross is
perched
on every tree branch in the city
At all times.
He has a voice like a schoolboy

Stop Hitting Yourself
Stop Hitting Yourself
Stop Hitting Yourself

He has a voice like a father.

Stand Up For Yourself
Stand Up For Yourself
Stand Up For Yourself

He has a voice like an older brother.

Fight Back
Fight Back
Fight back

My god, he is a republican.

Stop Being A Victim
Stop Being A Victim
Stop Being A Victim

You'll stop getting bullied
when you
stand up for yourself
fight back
stop being a victim
stop hitting yourself
stop hitting yourself

"Ok... Ok..."
        you tell Albatross
"Here. I want you to have this"
And you shoot him through his goddamn guts
with a crossbow made of your fists.

You grab Albatross by the heart
and punch him

until he resembles a mass of dirty red shirts.
Until he resembles a bloody mess.
Until he resembles you
and all the corpse he has made out of you.

Not like that!
Squawks Dead Albatross
Not like that!

"Oh, but Albatross.
I have stopped hitting myself
and I have started hitting you.

Oh but Albatross
I am standing up for myself
on top of your neck.

Oh, but Albatross
I am fighting back
see all this blood?
it isn't mine this time!"

But you're still a victim
Says Dead Albatross

"Oh, but Albatross,
So are you, now.
So you will be always.
And now hell is a place for both of us.

You have loved making a monster
out of me, Albatross.
And so you have earned my teeth.
You sharpened them yourself, Albatross"

When the world finds you-
you will have 2 broken hands.
you will be covered in bloody feathers.
They will see the dead Albatross
and despair-
What Have You Done!?
Why have you killed
such a beautiful bird?
Only a monster would do such a thing!
And they are right.

And they will crucify Dead Albatross
to your collarbone and shoulders.
you carry Albatross everywhere you go.
A tattoo of a dead friend.

Heavy as the ocean
And all the things it has swallowed.

You've been poisoned.
You can't stop hitting yourself.

Koga

You should have warned me
that your hair
was poison oak.
It would not have
made any difference
but still,
you should warn people
about the things
they will fall in love with.

My arms
and face
and neck
are on fire.
It feels as though
I am becoming
a burning tree
at some winter festival.
Fortunately for us,
there is no ointment
for you.

May this body
burn to ashes
without ever
finding the
cure.

Biker

That's the thing about gasoline.
It's poison,
but damn, it's our favorite one.

It's a big hit with kids like me.
Bigger than cigarettes.
But not quite so big as Jesus.
No.
Not quite so big as that.

Jesus was,
after all
the first tank of gas
we ever drank.

Burglar

One time
someone broke into my house
so I broke into their face
and found so much fear in there
that I made a fortune
selling it all on wall street.

Cue Ball

After losing all my hair
I said "fuck it"
and bought a codpiece,
a whip
and a motorcycle.

It was all a huge mistake.

Having acknowledged this,
I beg of you.
Please give me
joint custody.
I just want to see my daughter.

Tarot

You decide not to get a tarot reading
from the seeress
in the suspicious tent.
Then end up getting one anyway
though you still know that you decided not to.

How you feel about yourself:
You drew the four of shotguns.
this card in this position
indicates that your spine is a shotgun.
You reach for the trigger
a voice echos in your head
       "There is a time and a place for everything
       But not right now."

What you want most right now:
You drew the twentyteenth of coins.
You remember the prayers you spent in the arcade.
They were answered.
You immediately combust again.
You want to forgive yourself for all you've failed to do
and all you've done instead-
but the shotgun lodged in your back won't let you.

Your fears:
You draw the you card.
On the card you are smiling.
You do not know why at first
because nothing in the card has changed
and then you start bleeding
on the pier again
and the shotgun in your spine swallows your scream.

What is going for you:
You draw the Scary Horse Guy card.
He offers to buy you a drink.
You accept.
You have a great time.
you end up paying for your drink anyway.
Scary Horse Guy laughs
Looks at his scythe
and says "There is a time and a place for everything
but not right now."

What is going against you:
You draw the you card again.

It gives you a paper cut.
You bleed on the card.
The you that is in the card smiles wider.

The Likely Outcome:
You draw the tomorrow card.
It is great and terrible and it scares you more than the peir
or the bleeding smile you are wearing.
The seeress cackles
and it becomes tomorrow.
Scary horse guy rides by
and grins and says
"Nothing that happened will ever happen again
in the exact same way you experienced it.
That is why you will survive
For now."

Sabrina

So, I bent some spoons
and everyone said I was a witch.
So, naturally
I bent their necks
because I am a witch.

They spit the bible at me
and I make their bible
spit back at them.

They pry open the door
to my house,
and I make my door
pry open them.

I hear they are burning
little girls
for being too pretty
or too ugly
or too everything
to be anything but magic.

But I can see the future.
I can see the world they make
by destroying all the magic
they can
or cannot
find.

It is a world of tax returns
and report cards
and stock market crashes.

Oh, how their children will beg for magic.
Oh, how they will grow up and try to build magic from lightning.
Oh, how they will fail
and burn the world down as they try to escape.

They will deserve
every ounce of misery
they have burned themselves into.

Psychic

So, I bent some spoons
and now I can tell the future
by looking into the past
through the eyes of God.
And it's not looking good.

We all die and become trees
but since we are all assholes
the trees also become assholes
and pollinate all over our children
and that is why seasonal allergies are so bad
because fucking grandpa is a piece of shit tree.

Pokemaniac

First of all
I'd like to thank
all my friends
for coming out tonight
to see me perform.

Mr. Fluffernutter,
you've always been a good friend to me.

Squishy Bear
how long has it been? 10 years? 30?
I lost count when mom died.

DoodleSnort,
you saved me life that night
I can't thank you enough.

Madame Poof-Lion,
if it wasn't for you
I'd never have the courage to face the day.

And finally
the guest of honor
Danger McSnuggle-Face
of all my medications
you are by far the most effective.

Channeler

I've been eating dreams lately.
To be more specific
I've been eating the dreams
in which I die.

They taste like whiskey.
They hurt.
They're delicious.
I hate them.

These are Jokes

You approach the old
Half burned down burned down comedy club.
You find a notebook of jokes.
You read it.

I

Two rocks are sitting next to each other in the desert
one rock turns to the other and says
"Why are we even here?"
The other rock doesn't respond
because rocks don't talk.
The one rock just cries
always cries
when the other rock answers this way.

II

A Priest and an Atheist
walk into a bar
because they are alcoholics.
Bartender asks the Priest
"What'll it be."
The Priest says "Whiskey"
the Atheist says "Same"
Bartender asks
"Why always whiskey?"
The Priest says
"Because it gets me drunk
and I have to be drunk
to say some of the things I say."
The Atheist says
"Same."

III

Knock Knock
who's there

.

Your loneliness

.

.

.

Knock Knock

.

Leave me alone

.

.

.

Knock Knock Knock

.

I said leave me alone!

.

But that's exactly what I came here to do.

IV

What do you get when you cross
a prayer?

V

How many bricks does it take?
as many bricks as it takes.

VI

If a forest is a collection of trees,
and if a forest collected exactly two trees
and then one of the trees disintegrates in the forest
did it disintegrate in a forest at all?

VII

The Same Priest
and the Same Atheist
walk into a bar
in hell.
Bartender asks
"Who are you?"
The Same Priest responds
"John, the Priest"
The Same Atheist responds
"Same."
The Same Priest cries
Always cries
when the Same Atheist answers this way.

You close the book of jokes
and burn the rest of the comedy club down.
The fire is laughing.
It sounds just like you.

Blaine

I have too many questions?
I can't even give them away?
I tried, the other day
at the thrift store
I said
"I have an entire bucketfull
of questions?"

And they just looked at me?
Like they were waiting for the punchline?
Actually, now that I bring this up,
everyone looks at me like that?

When I say
"pass the salt?"
They look at me
like I should be passing
them the salt?
Sometimes they say
"No thank you"
and I think that's very rude?

When someone asks you something
you should respond appropriately?
And immediately?
especially when it's your elder
that is asking you?

Like, the other day,
I introduced myself
to a nice young lady?
I said "Hello? My name is Blaine?"

And I really thought we were
hitting it off?
She even said she would
drive me home?
But then she dropped me off
at an alzheimer's clinic?

And I said
"No? I don't have alzheimers?
I just have too many questions?
Please don't take me back there?"

But she did?
And the nurses tucked me in
like they always do?

Juggler

I'm an expert juggler.
I can juggle anything.
Balls,
bricks,
bowling pins,
the crushing feeling of never being good enough,
medications,
shotguns,
imposter syndrome,
and all these regrets

All at once.
Not even in that order.
With my goddamn broken hands.
What I'm trying to say is,
I'm fucking talented.
Give me money.

Gambler

They say,
gambling is a sin
as they put their money
in the collection plate
and let it ride.

I say,
better a gambler
than a beggar.
Better a beggar
than a thief.
Better a thief
than a religion,
which is all those things combined.

Bird Keeper

I wish I could be a bird.
Fly anywhere I wanted.
I envy their freedom.

Because I cannot be a bird,
I settle for the next best thing.
I put every bird I find
in a cage
just like mine.

Show and Tell

Hanging on the wall of the city
you find the shotgun
you were born holding.

when people look down the barrel
they see your dead great uncle
Looking back at them
Like a periscope.
Like suicide had captured him there.
He is all vietnam and wailing like his mother
So loud they'd say it was loaded.
Because it is.

When you aim down the sights,
Press your ear to the stock
You can hear him.
What he says is:
"It doesn't matter what you're aiming at.
What matters is
How you feel
When you aim it."

See the notches
carved into the barrel?
All those cuts
Have the same last name as you.
Each jagged slash
Like someone was punishing
The shotgun in their arms
For not being wings.

Bet you wanna know
Why the stock is shaped like a bottle.
Bet you wanna know
Why the hammer is shaped like a lover.
Bet you wanna know
Why the trigger
Is shaped like nothing
But a trigger.

You take it out of your backpack.
Your hand me down.
This family heirloom.
Sure is heavy, aint it?

and all the other kids say

"I wish my dad
Got me something this nice.
I wish I could trade
These blue eyes
For something this powerful."

Sometimes at Night,
you shiver so loud
All the shotgun shells fall out.
They all have your last name on them.

The words echo in your head
        "There's a time and a place for everything
but not now"
So you store it in your spine.

Giovanni

Dear son
I hope this letter
finds you on fire.

I hope you have
become the blaze
I always knew you could be.

You were always
the hottest red cherry
in my book of matches.

I would give you some advice
on how to burn the world down.
But my absence
has said more on the subject
than I ever could.

Besides
what would an old cigarette
like me
know of flames?

Don't ever start smoking
without first
bursting into flame.

Visiting hours
at the prison
are from noon to five.

Don't stop by.
I could not bare to see
what I looked like
before I became
this pile of ashes.

I had enough potential
to burn the world down.
And I did.
And I'll never forgive myself
for that.

Rocket Grunt

When it's one in the morning
and there is nobody to love
I want to sneak out into the neighborhoods
and steal everybody's weapons
like a reverse santa claus.

When they wake up
they won't be able to shoot each other
and they'll have to settle their grudges
with dance battles
and kissing contests
and riddles.

Then again,
maybe they'll just punch each other to death.
But that's ok with me.
It's so much easier
to fall in love
when nobody has a gun.

Cooltrainer

You don't become this cool
by having your shit together.

You become this cool
by binge drinking,
but never getting sick.

By driving drunk
but never crashing.

By doing all the wrong things
and never once getting hurt.

Look at me
I'm a wound that never bleeds.
The log the fire won't eat
doing so much cocaine
and never ever getting addicted.
It's not cool to be addicted.
It's much cooler to get your friends addicted.

Be so invincible
that all your friends die
trying to be you.

You become this cool
by being the most functional wreck
in the junkyard.

And if you've made it as far as me.
If you are exactly this cool,
you could run for office.

Indigo Plateau

You arrive at your destination
but they do not let you enter
without first passing
a citizenship test.

In the most godless part of Texas
there is a train.
This train is traveling at a speed of
ninety seven miles per hour.
It is headed west.
It is headed west
because it wants to get rich.
It wants to get famous.
It wants to load Los Angeles onto its back
and take it with.

Its cargo is aspirin
but it thinks that it is full of cocaine,
each bottle of aspirin contains
200 milligrams of gunpowder
and 100 milligrams of
"Good job kid,
you done a good job."
Which is why the train thinks
that the aspirin is actually cocaine.

On board
the conductor
is making 15
bucks an hour.
He dreams
of one day becoming a train
with a coal-fired heart
and clear direction.

The conductor has 3 kids.
None of them want to be conductors.
They are each a lightning bolt.
They all want to be grounded.
Because that would mean
that their father would be there to tell them so
to take them by the hand
to their rooms.

They all live in a stormcloud
with their mother.

Who is rain.
Four days a week
she fills her tea cups
with her raindrops
and sells them for 15 dollars each
to men who do not deserve them.

Answer the questions based on the above information.

1

How many raindrops does it take to fill one tea cup and how many tea cups does the rain
have to sell to put her lightning bolts through private school?
A. 20, 6000.
B. C
C. B
D. Our eyes contain enough rain to turn our voices into rivers and our chests contain enough
lightning to burn down our bodies.

You mark D. You don't know how expensive private school is. You don't know the volume of
a tea cup. But you learned exactly how much electricity it takes to burn a body down in Ce-
ladon City. And you learned exactly how deep a river must be to drown in when you visited
Cerulean City.

2

If the conductor travels from The Most Godless Part of Texas to LA, will the money he has made
be enough to afford living in a stormcloud? Would he have enough money to become a train
when he reaches LA?
A. True, Yes, and Forever.
B. False, No, and Never.
C. The conductor is already the train. He is its heart, mind and stomach. Trains do not need a
place to live, only a place to go.
D. Both A and B, but not D.

You mark B. It is not the answer you wanted to mark, but you think it is the answer the test
wants. You do not know where Texas and LA are. You have no idea what a conductor does
other than transfer power. A fact you learned in Vermillion City.

3

If the train sells enough cocaine in LA, could it afford acting lessons and/or a place to beat its
blues songs into the ears of important people, rather than the Texas dirt?
A. Tie your heart to the tracks, kid.
B. Press the coal in your gut into a diamond.
C. The cocaine will never sell because it is aspirin being sent to treat the heart attack that is
Hollywood.
D. All of the Above.

Scary Horse Guy, who is sitting in front of you, passes you a cheat sheet. It is a white Bic lighter. It
has a flame like a Lavender Town seance candle. Dead Albatross squawks and you hit yourself
with it gently. The burn mark smiles like a Pewter City cliffside and the shotgun in you is pleased.

You turn in your answer sheet.
you did not
understand
any of the questions
on the test.
But you are covered in lighter burns.
So they let you pass.

Lorelei

Behold the ice queen.
How I sit on my throne of skulls.
How I rule you like a kingdom.
How great and terrible am I
who does not care
that you love me.
How icy is this heart
that could do without your affection.

Must be a queen of the tundra,
you say.
How could I have mistaken a blizzard
for a woman
you say.

You shiver and tremble at the thought
that your heart does not matter to me
and, oh, what great power I wield over you
by finding you irrelevant.

And you cower and wonder
how this ice queen got so powerful.
Perhaps I was a witch
that was too cold to burn.
Perhaps I am haunted by a frozen ghost
and only need true love's kiss.

Or perhaps,
you just suck.
Oh no,
it couldn't be that.
That is just too factual
to be real.
More likely it is
some great and terrible magic.
More likely
I am a damsel to be saved
or a monster to be slain.

So, come with your sweet words
and follow with your threats.
Watch them slide off
like water droplets on ice
and watch your ego freeze to death.
And know that your fear is true.
That I have become so great and powerful
simply by not loving you.

Bruno

Let us play a game.

One statement will be the truth.
The other will be a lie.

My wife is in love with a mountain.
I once crushed a mountain using only my fists.

I am terrified of thunder.
I am in love with lightning.

I am, all of me, an oil spill.
I am so flammable, I dream of fire escapes.

I have never loved anything that has a name.
My name is Bruno, and it is my deepest regret.

Sometimes, I am an apartment with no windows.
Sometimes, I am a house with no doors, or beds, or people.

There is a man with no name, and he is my hero.
There is a man called father and he has no name.

My father is a lighthouse with no candle.
My father is a fire that produces no light, and it burns like shipwreck.

There is a stingray in my chest.
There is a shark in my blood and I've named it Loved One.

I have spent my life becoming a myth.
I have spent my life trying to become a lie.

I am a pretty fiction that all the boys fall in love with
I am an ugly truth and my gender is Fire.

Do you know
which statements were lies
son?
Can you tell the truth
when you see it
like a constellation on a clear night?

They are all of them
the truth
son.
Save for one.
When I told you there would be lies
well, I lied.

Agatha

Are you afraid of ghosts, child?
Do you fear the dead things in the darkness
or the noises they make in your dreams?

I collect ghosts, you know.
When you get to be
as old as I am
all your best friends will be ghosts.
All the boys you've loved
and all their blooming secrets
will also be ghosts.
I have quite the collection.

There is no need to fear that which you loved.
No, it is not death that quakes our knees at night.
The hides within the shadows.
It is Loss,
that lurking thing
with no head
and no anything.
That is what we fear so badly
that we hold stuffed beasts
in self defense.

But when loss bites,
and eats your dreams
as you sweat in bed,
it can do you no more harm.

I once loved an oak tree that ate dead things
and little girls.
He was strong and yong
and I was romanced by his hunger
for corpses
like me.

But Loss,
that creeping, nibbling thing
made a nest in his heart.
I was so scared.
I prayed that he would live forever.
Then I prayed that he would die quietly
and far away
where Loss could not bite me.
I'm not sure if my prayer was answered.
And that terrifies me
more than any ghost.

Lance

The great dragon tamer Lance
who has not yet screamed the dirt into a grave.
What a hero is he
who has charmed the beast in his blood
with steel and stone.

There's a dragon
in my bloodstream.
Its name is Anxiety
and it is full of rage
and it is a fire made of my flesh
and it is my god.

I am no dragon tamer.
If such a thing were possible
then worms would tame birds.
No, I do not tame dragons.
I am a dragon.

I became one by swallowing my regrets like klonopin
and sleeping as I burn.

I became a dragon
by collecting my broken hearts like treasure
and guarding my horde
with all the fire and razor in me.

Hi, my name is Lance.
I was born with a dragon in my bones
and now it is in my blood, and now it is my whole self
and I don't know what else to do but breathe fire
and never love anybody.
All these scars n my forearms, and wrists, and legs
are actually scales,
now I don't even bleed the same
so I don't know what to do anymore.

Hello, if you're reading this message
then please send knights, or a hero, or a hangman
to slay this beast that I become when I hurt.
Or when I am about to hurt. Or when I want to hurt.
Which is all the time.

But please,
I beg of you.
Don't send anything beautiful.
Don't send anything
I could fall in love with.

Rival

I wanted to be the very best
like noone ever was.
But instead, I just became noone.
The champion of poems
about death and nothing.

And now, you've come.
You've collected the rocks
and learned how they learned their secrets.
Did you find them at the bottom
of the great black sea,
like I did?
While you were down there,
did you fall in love with the ghosts
and the trees that eat them?
Did you hear the song
all the dead soldiers sing?
It is my favorite lullaby.
I'm sure that it's yours too.
Sing me to sleep with it.
I will return the favor.

We will fall asleep?
And when we wake up?
All the poems will be dead?
And the world will have burned down?
And you will have taken my place as champion?

We will, once again, live in a world
of tax returns
and report cards
and stock market crashes.

The ice queens will fall in love.
The liars will tell the truth.
The ghosts will go back to their graves.
And the dragons will fly south
and never come back.

When we learn of this
we will never forgive ourselves
for letting it happen.

But still,
I think it is the most beautiful thing
we could possibly do
for each other.
Let these poems die inside of us.

Because they will be so much better
as memories.

So, let us sing

Halfway down the road to hell
lies a place where dead things dwell
Their sins are many
yet their sins are clean
those trainers there, at Fiddler's Green

with love
-RJ

Praise for Indigo League

"Trainers of Kanto* is the instruction manual with which RJ Walker guides us through the Pokemon world, stripped of all that distinguishes it from our own. The world is a closet lined with too familiar costumes– the forlorn lover, the bishop's robe, the peach, the burglar mask, the heirloom, the witch's dress, the doctor, the medicated patient– and he deftly tunnels through them like video game levels. Inside each costume is another costume, then another, then another, and finally lands upon a rock or wedding ring or this heavy book that shifts between the two with uncomfortable ease. Trainers "is not a rock, it's a door", one that leads us back to ourselves by rehearsing all the roles we already know by heart. It is a memorable seminar in what video game lovers already know: to escape into the relief of another world, you have to learn the pain of this one. You have to navigate this new one, with this new body, with the old ones breathing down your neck."
- 'Good Ghost' Bill Moran

As a die-hard fan of Pokémon games, I expected to love Trainers of Kanto*, but I didn't expect to find such an emotional gut-punch. In this collection, RJ provides a master class in the economy of words, crafting concise, brilliant, direct narratives that will inspire readers with their emotional weight, regardless of whether the reader has any familiarity with the source material. RJ creates worlds, lives, and stories that stand on their own as a cohesive, self-reflective collection that reminds me of Edgar Lee Masters' Spoon River Anthology in its adept poetic ability and its careful attention to character. RJ will take you through a journey of pain, humor, wit, love, loss, and humanity, and I will forever envy his ability to do so in such masterful strokes, setting up clear characters in just a few lines, and then leaving his reader reeling one line later. This is easily one of my favorite chapbooks I have read in some time, and I'm sure that feeling will be shared by anyone who comes across this collection.
- Patrick Roche

*Called 'Trainers of Kanto' when reviewed

RJ Walker

RJ Walker is a performance poet from Salt Lake City, Utah. RJ Has performed at the national poetry slam five times representing Salt Lake City, and Sugar House Utah. He has also represented Sugar House and Salt Lake at the Individual world poetry slam, where he was a showcased poet on final stage. He is currently ranked 6th in the world of slam poetry. He is the host and operator of The Greenhouse Effect Open Mic, SLC's longest running and most popular open mic style event. Videos of his work have been published by PSI, Write About Now, and Button Poetry.

He operates a poetry subscritpion service at
www.patreon.com/dollarcompliments
and more of his books can be found at
www.rjwalker.bandcamp.com

Made in the USA
Columbia, SC
30 July 2019